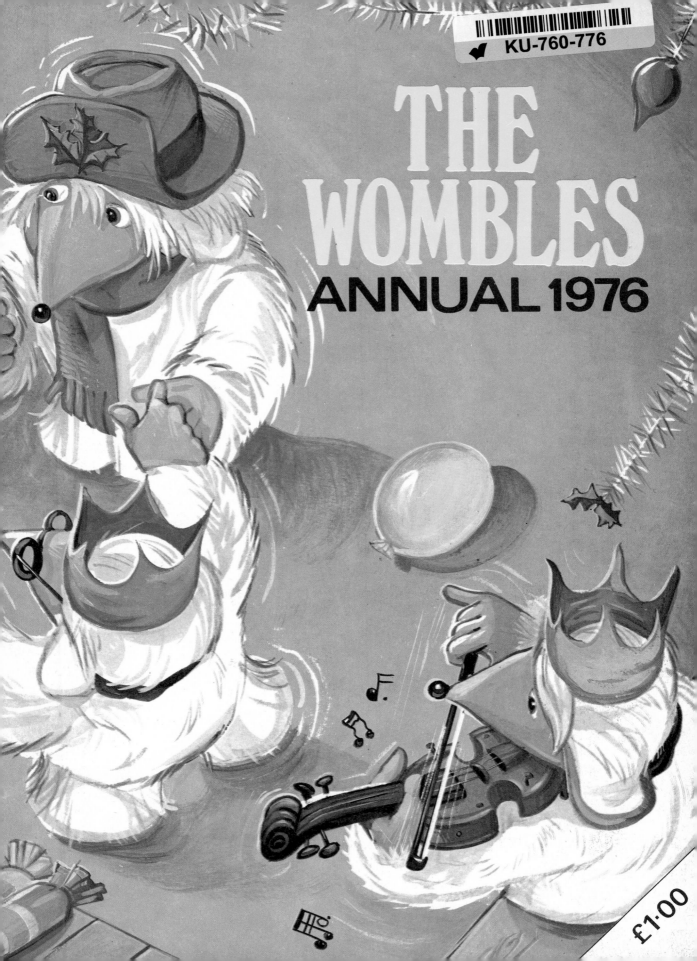

THE WOMBLES
ANNUAL 1976

£1·00

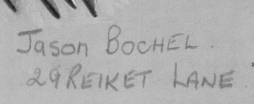

contents

**Drawn from Ivor Wood's original
film puppets by David Fryer.**

Copyright © MCMLXXV by
Wombles Limited/Filmfair Limited

Based on the BBC-TV series.

Original text and character material
© Elisabeth Beresford.
Original film puppet designs by
Ivor Woods © Filmfair Limited.

All rights reserved throughout the world.

Published in Great Britain by
World Distributors (Manchester) Limited.
P.O. Box 111, 12 Lever Street,
Manchester M60 1TS.

Printed in Great Britain by
Jarrold and Sons Limited, Norwich.

SBN 7235 0306 0

ORINOCO-RIP-VAN-WOMBLE

"Where's Orinoco?" asked Bungo. "I haven't seen him doing any tidying-up work on the Common for the last three days!"

"I haven't seen him at all," said Tomsk, "not even when I've been doing my running exercises round the Common. Perhaps he's become invisible!"

"No, he hasn't," said Wellington in his quiet voice, "because I know where he's been. Oh dear, perhaps I shouldn't tell. It's not fair to tell tales about other Wombles."

Tomsk and Bungo both looked at Wellington, who was shuffling his feet and wiping his big, round spectacles on the end of his scarf.

"Yes, it *is* fair," said Bungo, "because we've got to know where he is in case there's something wrong with him!"

"Oh, Orinoco is all right," replied Wellington cheerfully. "He's made himself a nice, cosy bed right in the middle of a big clump of bushes near Queen's Mere, and every morning he goes along there and settles down and has a nice forty winks. He told me that the winter weather makes him feel very sleepy, you know."

Bungo and Tomsk looked at each other and shook their heads. Really it was too bad of Orinoco to slide out of doing his share of the tidying-up work. He was such a lazy young Womble, and it was high time that somebody taught him a lesson!

The three young Wombles put their heads together, but they couldn't think of a way which would make Orinoco stop being so lazy. However, that evening, before they went to bed, Great Uncle Bulgaria read them a story called *Rip Van Winkle.* It was a very interesting story about a man who went to sleep for a hundred years so that when he woke up he was extremely

old and he had a long white beard and was covered in cobwebs.

"My goodness," said Orinoco, "fancy going to sleep for a hundred years! That must be as long as forty winks and forty winks AND forty winks AND . . . ."

"I shouldn't like to do it," said Bungo.

"I would," said Orinoco, with an enormous yawn. "I think it'd be lovely. Well, I'm off to bed. It's been a very hard day, you know."

And off went Orinoco, exactly as if he *had* been working all day.

"Hang on," said Bungo to Wellington and Tomsk, "I've got an idea. I've got a SMASHING idea. I know how we'll teach Orinoco not to be so lazy. Come here and I'll explain."

Bungo began to whisper to the other two young Wombles, and they listened to what he had to say with their eyes as round as marbles, and then they laughed and laughed.

Early next morning, before they went off on tidying-up work, Wellington went to see Madame Cholet in the kitchen and asked her for a mug of flour. Bungo visited Tobermory in the Workshop and asked him for some of the old odds and ends of white and grey knitting wool which had been picked up on the Common. While, as for Tomsk, he went and borrowed a net curtain which was on the washing line.

The three young Wombles put all these strange bits and pieces into their tidy-bags and then, trying not to laugh, they joined Orinoco for breakfast.

"I tell you what," said Orinoco, "I'll tidy up the bit of the Common which is near Queen's Mere. It's quite a big bit, so it's jolly nice of me to do it really. Cheerio for now, see you at dinner-time."

Off went Orinoco, swinging his tidy-bag and whistling to himself.

It was a nice sharp, sunny morning and he really felt very cheerful. He picked up a couple of paper bags and some bus tickets and a few sweet wrappers and then he said to himself, "Well that's a *lot* of work done. I think I deserve a nice little nap to get my strength up again. It's just the morning for a cosy forty winks."

Orinoco looked to left and right with his sharp little eyes. But he couldn't see anybody else about and then, with a burst of speed surprising in a Womble of his fat, round shape, he scrambled through the bushes until he reached the comfortable bed of bracken and gorse that he had made for himself earlier in the week.

"How very tempting, how very cosy," said Orinoco. He plumped up his tidy-bag, put it under his head as a pillow, folded his paws across his fat little stomach, and within two minutes he was fast asleep.

"Zzzzzzzzzz," said Orinoco. "Zzzzzzzzz."

Perhaps he wouldn't have slept so soundly if he had realised that ever since he had left the Burrow, Tomsk, Bungo and Wellington had been following him very, very carefully. They hadn't made a sound, and when Orinoco had looked round they had fallen flat on their faces behind some bushes.

"Right," whispered Bungo. "This is what we do . . . ."

First Bungo very, very quietly sprinkled some flour over the sleeping Orinoco. Then Wellington, with his neat little paws, wound some of the white wool round Orinoco's ears and across his chin. Finally Tomsk spread the white net curtain over the bushes which surrounded Orinoco.

They had to stop then so that they could chuckle behind their paws.

"Doesn't he look funny?" whispered Tomsk.

"He looks as old as Great Uncle Bulgaria," snorted Bungo.

"He's Great Uncle Orinoco now," wheezed Wellington.

And that made them laugh so much that they had to hide behind a tree for at least ten minutes until they could be quiet again.

"Now us," whispered Bungo, and the three Wombles dusted down their fur with what was left of the flour and made themselves long white beards of knitting wool. Tomsk found three pieces of wood and they leant on them like walking sticks.

"It's time to wake up Rip-Van-Orinoco," said Bungo. "Come on!"

They crept forward and looked down at the sleeping Orinoco, who was still snoring gently with a happy smile on his round white face.

"Ahhhhh, there he is," said Bungo in a loud, quavering voice. "At long last we've found him again. Wake up old friend."

He gave Orinoco a jab with his walking stick.

Orinoco stirred and turned on his side.

Bungo gave him another jab, and very slowly Orinoco opened his eyes and said in a sleepy voice.

"What is it? What's the matter? Is it dinner-time?"

"Dinner-time?" quavered Bungo. "How can you worry about dinner when you've been asleep for so long? Surely you can't be hungry?

Oh, how good it is to find you again."

Orinoco opened his eyes very wide indeed at these strange words and he stared and stared and STARED at the three, bent white Wombles with their long beards who were standing round him.

"Why do you look so old, What, what, what's happened?" asked

Orinoco in a faint voice.

"You've woken up at last, *that's* what's happened," said Wellington, making his voice very old and shaky. "You've been asleep for years and years and YEARS. Look at your white fur, look at your long beard, look at that enormous net – I mean spider's web, on the bushes."

Orinoco looked and then he looked again. He saw his young friends looking even older than Great Uncle Bulgaria. He saw that his own fur had turned white and that he had a long white beard which came right down over his tummy.

"It's very good to see you wide awake again," said Bungo.

"We've missed you all these years," said Tomsk, shaking his white head. "And *you've* missed all those delicious dinners and teas and breakfasts that Madame Cholet's cooked."

"Ooooooooooh," wailed Orinoco, "I only meant to have a nice 40 winks, not a nice *40,000* winks. I'll never have a nap again. NEVER! At least not while I'm meant to be working."

"You've missed a hundred years of work too, don't forget," said Bungo.

"I'll make it up," said Orinoco, and with a speed surprising in a Womble of his 'Great Age' he bounded off his bracken bed, took hold of his tidy-bag and pushed his way through the bushes. He began to work harder and faster than he had ever done before in his whole lazy, young life!

Of course Bungo, Tomsk and Wellington weren't going to go *on* pretending that Orinoco had slept for a hundred years . . . but as it happened Orinoco discovered the trick they had played on him before he got back to the burrow. How? Well, the flour came off his fur, he soon found out that his beard was made of wool, and he realised that the net curtain was NOT an enormous spider's web after all.

However, Orinoco had had rather a fright, but he took the trick his friends had played on him in good part, so much so that for at least a whole week he really did work hard.

And even now if he slackens off badly and tries to slide away for a little nap, somebody has only got to whisper, How's Orinoco Rip-Van-Womble today, then?"

And Orinoco sighs deeply, reaches for his tidy-bag and ambles off to look for some rubbish.

But, knowing Orinoco, the day is sure to come when he'll make himself a nice, cosy comfortable secret little bed *somewhere* on Wimbledon Common, so that he can have a much needed forty winks in perfect peace and quiet.

All about the WOMBLES

If you can answer all these questions correctly you are a real Wombles fan, and you will be very welcome on Wimbledon Common to help the Wombles keep everything tidy.

1. Who is the head of the British Wombles?

2. Which Womble has a wonderful workshop?

3. Who is the nightwatch Womble?

4. Which Womble helps Madame Cholet in her kitchen?

5. Which is the fattest and laziest Womble of all?

6. Which Womble cousin once went to see the tennis at Wimbledon?

7. Which Womble went to London's Piccadilly to search for his Womble friend who had run away?

8. What is Great Uncle Bulgaria's middle name?

9. What did the Wombles give their friend Mr. Smith for Christmas?

10. What was the name of the Womble Cousin Yellowstone met in Bombay?

How did you do? Check your answers on page 60

WELLINGTON WOMBLE,
WEATHER FORECASTER

As you probably know, Wellington Womble is never quite so happy as when he has a good book to read. It doesn't matter what sort of book it is, he reads all different kinds.

One of his favourite books is one that he read recently on forecasting the weather, and he was so impressed with one or two of the things mentioned in it that he decided to draw up a chart to be hung on one of the burrow walls.

He's sent a copy for you too, so that you can forecast the weather, and it's quite easy when you know how . . . or, at least, Wellington thinks so.

If you hear a donkey braying or see cattle in a field lying down then you can be fairly certain that there's wet weather on the way.

Corns begin to ache if there's bad weather on the way. Wellington believes that Great Uncle Bulgaria could say whether this is true or not, but he really doesn't like asking.

Birds returning to the trees in great numbers means that there's a storm on the way, unless of course there's a cat around, in which case it means something completely different . . . .

Crickets chirp faster in warmer weather, in fact, you can even tell how hot it is by counting how many chirps a cricket has made in fifteen seconds and then adding thirty-seven to that number. But you'll have to listen carefully . . . .

GREAT UNCLE BULGARIA LOOPS the LOOP

"Don't do this, don't do that, talk quietly, make your bed properly!" said Bungo. "That's all that Great Uncle Bulgaria says these days. If you ask me he's getting old and fussy."

"*Shhh,* he'll hear you," said Wellington.

"I don't care if he does," said Bungo – which wasn't strictly true. "If you ask *me*, Great Uncle Bulgaria's got so old he's forgotten what it's like to be a young Womble and to want to do exciting things!"

Bungo was feeling cross because he had been ticked off several times in the last few days for doing all kinds of silly, if exciting things. The latest of these had been to make a large box kite with Tomsk's help. They had certainly been very noisy while they were doing it, and they had happened to use a sheet off Bungo's bed for the sides of the kite.

"Nobody," thought Bungo, "could have realised that the kite would go straight up into the sky very fast indeed," even though Bungo was attached to its tail at the time. So, of course, he had done the most sensible thing and let go. And it was just bad luck that he had landed on the roof of the burrow and shaken down some plaster, and even worse luck that the kite had then got caught in a tree and the sheet had become rather torn.

"I only wanted to see what flying was like," Bungo said sulkily. "It's not my fault if Great Uncle Bulgaria doesn't want to do nice, exciting things like flying. If you ask me . . ."

And so on and so on, until all the other Wombles were sick and tired of hearing him grumbling. All the other Wombles, that is, except Great Uncle Bulgaria, and quite suddenly he *did* feel rather old and unadventurous. He looked at his white fur in the mirror and the wrinkles round his nose and he sighed. Once upon a time he too had had all kinds of ideas for adventures. Why, when he'd been young he had gone up in balloons and, because he had enjoyed it so much, he had later learnt to fly.

"Dear me," said Great Uncle Bulgaria suddenly, "I do believe I've still got the address of that Flying Club. I think I'll pay them a visit."

For the next week Great Uncle Bulgaria behaved in such a strange way that Tobermory and Madame Cholet got quite worried about him. He kept going off for long walks, without telling anyone where he was going, and he picked out an old leather coat and some goggles and a knitted hat from the Workshop.

But he wouldn't say what he needed them for or what he was up to. It was all most mysterious.

However, at the end of the week a notice was pinned on Great Uncle Bulgaria's study door. It said,
FLYING TOMORROW.
COME AND WATCH!
(ESPECIALLY BUNGO!!)

As the Wombles are the most inquisitive creatures in the world they were all very interested in this, and next morning, bright and early, they were all lined up outside the burrow looking up at the sky. There was nothing to see, except for a few little white clouds, until over the horizon appeared a very strange looking object. It wasn't a bird and it wasn't a plane, but something between the two.

"It's – it's a very old-fashioned bi-plane," said Tobermory. "Dear me, I didn't know there were any left. It must be very old and not at all safe. Who can possibly be flying *that*?"

Nearer and nearer came this strange object. It didn't travel very fast and it bumped up and down quite a bit in a way which made the young Wombles feel quite air-sick.

"I wouldn't fly in *that*," said Bungo. "It doesn't look safe at all . . ."

"It's higher than our kite went," said Tomsk.

"But look who's sitting in it!" whispered Wellington.

"It's Great Uncle Bulgaria," replied Orinoco. "And *he's* flying it! Oh dear!"

They all stared up at the funny looking plane, almost unable to believe their round little eyes. But it quite obviously *was* Great Uncle Bulgaria sitting up there in the sky wearing an old leather coat, a pair of goggles and a knitted hat.

He had seen them too, for he suddenly waved one white paw and then, before they could get their breath back, he did the most extraordinary thing. He zoomed down out of the sky and straight at them.

Everybody stood there for about ten seconds, and then they turned and ran in all directions, because it was most alarming seeing this strange, bumpy object zooming at them.

'Zip, *zzzzzzap, whoom* and over,' said Great Uncle Bulgaria to himself, and he did the most perfect loop-the-loop right over the burrow. He enjoyed it so much that he did it again and then a third time for luck. Really, what fun it was to do something adventurous and silly for a change! Perhaps he could get some of the young Wombles to join him on his next flight. . . .

But the strange thing was that when Great Uncle Bulgaria, who

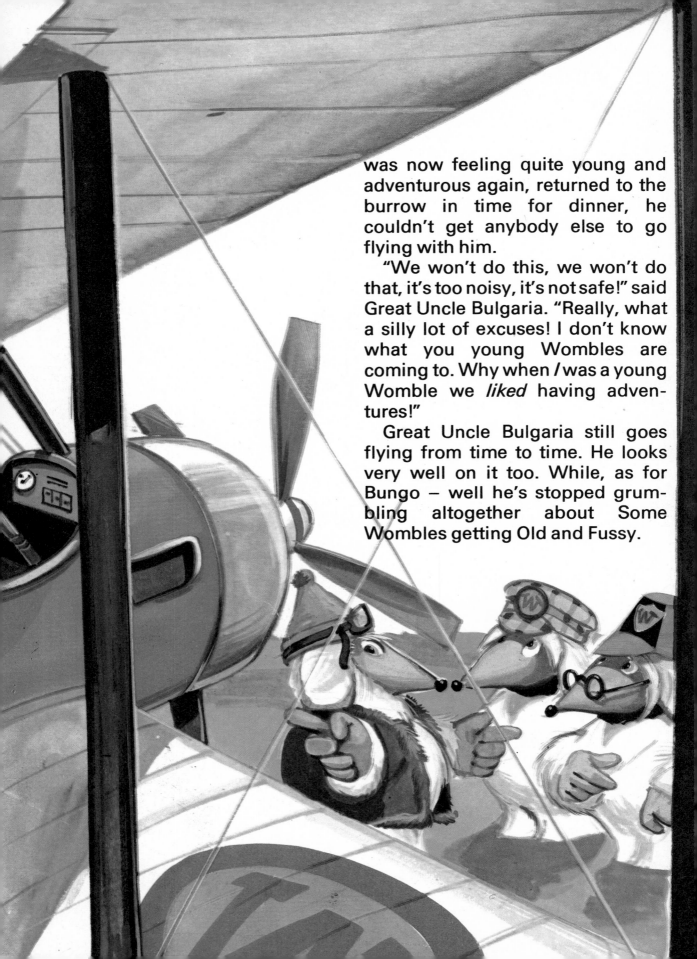

was now feeling quite young and adventurous again, returned to the burrow in time for dinner, he couldn't get anybody else to go flying with him.

"We won't do this, we won't do that, it's too noisy, it's not safe!" said Great Uncle Bulgaria. "Really, what a silly lot of excuses! I don't know what you young Wombles are coming to. Why when *I* was a young Womble we *liked* having adventures!"

Great Uncle Bulgaria still goes flying from time to time. He looks very well on it too. While, as for Bungo – well he's stopped grumbling altogether about Some Wombles getting Old and Fussy.

TOBERMORY'S workshop

There's scarves and socks, and coats and hats,
Sunshades and brollies, cloths and mats,
Piles of money from near and far,
And nuts and bolts to mend a car.

Bags and baskets for Wombles all,
Books and papers old days recall.
And girl Wombles who like to sew,
Find cotton reels all in a row.

There are games too for a rainy day,
When indoors small Wombles have to stay,
And jars, for Madame Cholet's jam,
And herbs, like basil and marjoram.

Everything's clearly labelled too,
So that it may be quickly found for you
By Tobermory, who's the best
Mechanical Womble, and the cleverest!

HAPPY CHRISTMAS

Last Christmas, Bungo and Orinoco were on the last minute as usual; all the other Wombles had made their Christmas presents for the others well in advance, but those two still had two presents to make on Christmas Eve. Finally they went to Tobermory and explained their problem: they still had two presents to make, one for Uncle Bulgaria and one for Madame Cholet, and they just didn't know what to do.

Tobermory had the answer right away. He suggested that they made an apron for Madame Cholet and a desk set for Uncle Bulgaria and that's what they did. And just in case you'd like to make one or other of them for someone you like, Tobermory has sent the instructions along.

Uncle Bulgaria's Desk Set

You'll need:
A clean empty cocoa or coffee tin
A new notebook
Some brightly-coloured sticky-backed plastic
A pair of scissors .
A few pencils and pens

All you have to do is cut out enough plastic to cover the tin (measure it carefully before cutting) and enough plastic to cover the front of the notebook. Then pull off the sticky backing on the plastic and cover the tin and notebook, making sure that it hasn't got any wrinkles in it or bubbles of air underneath.

Then fill up the tin with a selection of pens and pencils and your matching desk set is complete and ready to give. Uncle Bulgaria was most pleased with his!

An Apron for Madame Cholet

You'll need:
A pretty teatowel with patterns on both sides
Some tape
A needle and cotton

First shape the top of the tea towel and sew firmly down to make the bib part: see our illustrations. Then turn up the bottom of the towel about four inches to form a pocket. Sew the 'pocket' in place down either side, and then sew a line of stitching up the centre to divide the pocket in two. Now sew some tape in a loop at the top of the bib, to go round the neck, and then sew a piece of tape at either side of the apron, so that the person can tie them round her waist . . . and you're finished!

Madame Cholet was so happy with her apron that she wore it to cook the Wombles' Christmas dinner. But, do remember, most tea towels are quite small, so an apron like this will only fit a little person.

A picnic for the WOMBLES

The Wombles were delighted when Great Uncle Bulgaria, Tobermory and Madame Cholet arranged a picnic for them all one warm summer's day. Here they are, all enjoying themselves, and just look at Orinoco dropping in from the sky! If you look closely at the picnic party picture, you will see lots of objects beginning with the letter P. There are at least ten . . . how many can you spot?

The MacWomble comes to stay

All the Wombles were very excited because they had just heard that their distant cousin Cairngorm, The MacWomble the Terrible from Scotland, was going to pay them a visit. The MacWomble is rather a fierce sort of Womble with his bushy red fur and loud voice and some of the young Wombles couldn't help wondering if he was going to be a bit frightening.

"Nonsense," said Great Uncle Bulgaria, "you'll have a wonderful time when The MacWomble arrives. We all will! Now then, I want some volunteers to help smarten up the Burrow. We've got to have it looking really bright and clean for The MacWomble. Orinoco, you can sweep down the passage."

Orinoco groaned.

"Tomsk, you can put up some fresh newspaper on the walls," went on Great Uncle Bulgaria.

Tomsk sighed.

"Bungo, you can polish the front door," continued Great Uncle Bulgaria.

"Oh dear," muttered Bungo.

"And as for you, Wellington," added great Uncle Bulgaria, "you can tidy up all the Common round the front of the Burrow."

Wellington didn't say anything at all.

"Quick, sharp!" ordered Great Uncle Bulgaria, clapping his paws together, and off he went to have a word with Madame Cholet about the special party food for The MacWomble's visit.

So for the next few days everybody in the Burrow was very busy indeed making it as smart as possible. Outside on the Common there was a lot happening, too. There seemed to be more rubbish than ever to collect as the weather was rather windy.

"I sometimes wish you young Wombles wouldn't tidy up quite so much," grumbled Tobermory as another load of rubbish was tipped onto his Workshop floor. "You keep making the place look like a rubbish dump. Now what can I do with a whole pile of old plastic tubes and plastic bags?"

"Here's a nice cushion I've just tidied up," said Orinoco, adding cheekily, "why don't you sit down for a while on that, Tobermory, while you work out what to do with all the rest of the litter!"

Tobermory picked up the cushion and was just going to throw it at Orinoco when Wellington came running in, saying: "Help, help. There's an awful monster on the far side of the Common and it's coming straight towards the Burrow. It's making a dreadful wailing howling noise!"

"Stuff and nonsense!" said Tobermory. "I don't believe a word of it. Still, hang on, young Womble, I'll go and get Great Uncle Bulgaria and we'll *all* have a look at this 'monster' of yours together!"

Five minutes later all the Wombles were standing outside the front door of the Burrow with their hands to their ears. What Wellington had said was quite true, for there really was the most awful howling, wailing sound and, what was more, it was getting closer all the time! The four young Wombles all took refuge behind Madame Cholet who was holding her largest rolling pin, for she was quite determined that no 'monster' was going to get as far as her kitchen.

"It's not a monster is it, Bulgaria?" asked Tobermory in a whisper.

"Of course not," said Great Uncle Bulgaria, who of all of them was not

in the least worried. "What we can hear is the – er – wonderful sound of the Scottish bagpipes. I think our cousin The MacWomble the Terrible must be approaching." Great Uncle Bulgaria lowered his voice and added in Tobermory's ear, "Usually the bagpipes produce really stirring, musical music. Perhaps The MacWomble doesn't play them very well! Ah, here he comes. . . ."

Round a clump of bushes appeared a rather fierce looking Womble, wearing a tartan cap with a silver 'W' on it, a kilt and boots. Clasped in his arms were the bagpipes which he was playing very loudly, and not very musically. He marched right up to the Burrow, gave a final blast on the pipes, and then there was a kind of moaning sound as he stopped playing and in the sudden, very pleasant, silence everybody, including The MacWomble, took a deep breath.

"Welcome to the Wimbledon Burrow, MacWomble the Terrible," said Great Uncle Bulgaria, holding out his paw.

"Thanks, but call me Cousin Cairngorm for short, do," said The MacWomble, in a voice which was almost as loud as his bagpipes. "I'm verra glad to see you all looking so bonny! And I'm verra glad to be here, although I feel a wee bit homesick for my own Loch Ness Burrow! I've had a wee bit of trouble with my pipes. They're not playing well."

"So we heard. Ahem. I mean . . .

oh dear," said Great Uncle Bulgaria politely. "Do come in and have some of the dinner which Madame Cholet has been cooking specially for you. Perhaps, Tobermory, *you* could mend the pipes so that they work better?"

All that evening, after the special dinner – which was extra delicious – Tobermory was busy in his Workshop. And so were Bungo, Wellington, Orinoco and Tomsk, for Tobermory had found a very special use for all the rubbish they had brought in from the Common.

"I don't think Cousin Cairngorm's frightening at all," said Bungo, "but then I never did anyway. Not like you others!"

Which wasn't strictly true but, luckily for Bungo, Wellington, Orinoco and Tomsk were too busy to argue with him.

Early next morning The Mac-Womble hopped out of bed and went for a little stroll on the Common. The truth of the matter was that he was feeling not just 'a wee' bit homesick, but very homesick indeed, for his home up by Loch Ness was hundreds of miles away from Wimbledon.

"It's aye quiet here," he muttered to himself.

Then he stopped, for the early morning hush was suddenly broken by the most dreadful howling, wailing din. It grew louder and louder and LOUDER, and then out of the Burrow marched the four young Wombles, all puffing and blowing and trying to play the oddest looking bagpipes. They were made out of the plastic pipes and bags from the Workshop. Behind them came Tobermory, carrying Cousin Cairngorm's own pipes, which had been mended quite beautifully. And behind Tobermory was Great Uncle Bulgaria – wearing large ear-muffs made out of the cushion which Orinoco had found.

"Good morning, Cousin Cairngorm," said Great Uncle Bulgaria, "and welcome to your very own pipe band. I hope you won't feel homesick any longer!"

"That I won't," agreed Cousin Cairngorm, beaming from ear to ear. "But I think I'd best take them well away from the Burrow to give them some practice. Thank you kindly, Tobermory."

Away went The MacWomble, playing for all he was worth, with the four young Wombles piping and wailing behind him.

"Now I know why he's called The MacWomble the Terrible," murmured Great Uncle Bulgaria. "It's because of the TERRIBLE din of those pipes. But perhaps I'll get used to them in time." And, adjusting his ear-muffs, he hastily re-entered the Burrow for a bit of peace and quiet before the return of Wimbledon Common's firstever Womble Bagpipe Band.

UNCLE BULGARIA'S SCRAPBOOK

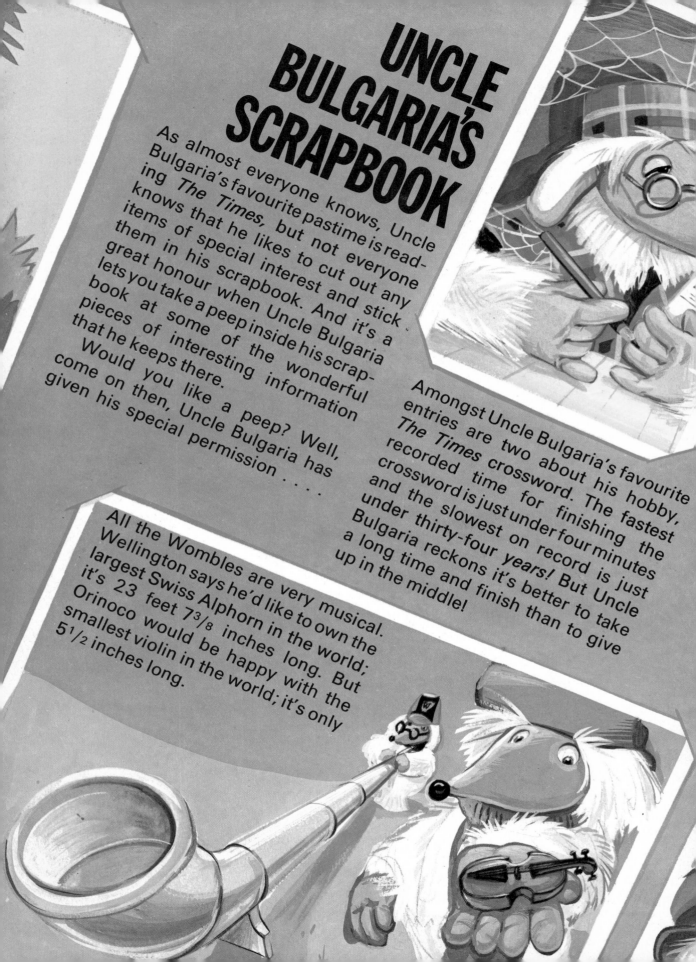

As almost everyone knows, Uncle Bulgaria's favourite pastime is reading *The Times*, but not everyone knows that he likes to cut out any items of special interest and stick them in his scrapbook. And it's a great honour when Uncle Bulgaria lets you take a peep inside his scrapbook at some of the wonderful pieces of interesting information that he keeps there.

Would you like a peep? Well, come on then, Uncle Bulgaria has given his special permission . . . .

Amongst Uncle Bulgaria's favourite entries are two about his hobby. *The Times* crossword. The fastest recorded time for finishing the crossword is just under four minutes and the slowest on record is just under thirty-four *years*! But Uncle Bulgaria reckons it's better to take a long time and finish than to give up in the middle!

All the Wombles are very musical. Wellington says he'd like to own the largest Swiss Alphorn in the world; it's 23 feet 7³/₈ inches long. But Orinoco would be happy with the smallest violin in the world; it's only 5¹/₂ inches long.

Tobermory is more interested in travelling, he'd like to travel all over the world, but most of all he'd like to see the largest pyramid ever built. And it's not in Egypt! The largest pyramid in the world is to be found 63 miles outside Mexico City, Mexico. It is 177 feet tall and its base covers nearly 45 acres. All the other Wombles are glad it wasn't built on Wimbledon Common!

When the Silver Womble gets crowded and all the little Wombles complain about getting squashed, Uncle Bulgaria reminds them all of the record number of people that a car has managed to carry – 103!

Orinoco and Madame Cholet wish that they'd been able to see and taste the largest cake in the world. It was a six-sided birthday cake baked in 1962 in Seattle, Washington, for the Seattle World's Fair. The cake was 23 feet high and 60 feet all the way round and it contained 10,500 pounds of flour, 4,000 pounds of sugar, 7,000 pounds of raisins, 2,200 pounds of nuts, 18,000 eggs and 100 pounds of salt. Orinoco gets hungry just thinking about it!

THE NAME GAME

BULGARIA is the wild, mountainous country beside Yugoslavia and Rumania. It has lovely hot summers, but cold snowy winters. In winter the people who live there like to stay inside their little wooden houses and eat their favourite foods of beans, rice and yogurt.

I'm sure many of you will already know that when the Wombles are old enough to choose names for themselves they get out Great Uncle Bulgaria's *Great Atlas of the World* and they each pick a name they like from there. You may not know much, however, about some of the strange-sounding places after which the Wombles are called. Perhaps you would like to get out your own atlas, and we will find together Bulgaria, Tobermory, Orinoco, Wellington and Alderney.

TOBERMORY is on the northern coast of the Island of Mull in Scotland. It is a seaside and fishing town, and some people say there's a sunken Spanish galleon somewhere off the coast. As these ships usually carried riches and treasure, that would be a good catch for someone.

ORINOCO isn't a place, but a river running through Venezuela in South America. It is in fact one of the longest, mightiest rivers in the world, and large parts of it are very dangerous for people in boats, because the water rushes so fast and energetically – well, that doesn't sound much like *our* Orinoco, does it?

WELLINGTON is the main city of New Zealand. New Zealand is made up of two islands, and Wellington is at the bottom of the top island. Built round a pretty harbour, the city has two cathedrals, a well-known university, an art gallery, a museum and several libraries – which was a good choice for scholarly Wellington who, of course, likes reading most of all the Wombles.

ALDERNEY is one of the Channel Islands which belong to Britain but lie just off the French coast. Womble Alderney is, of course, Madame Cholet's assistant – and she is every bit as pretty as the tiny island whose name she shares.

35

WELLINGTON'S CROSSWORD

One day Wellington was in bed with a cold. To stop himself from becoming bored, Wellington decided to invent a crossword puzzle all about the Wombles. Can you solve it?

ACROSS

1. Which Womble looks after the Workshop?
6. What sort of a book did the Wombles choose their names from?
8. How many lady Wombles are there?
9. Who is the greediest, fattest and laziest Womble?
11. Because Great Uncle Bulgaria feels the cold very badly he usually wears a tartan _ _ _ _ _ to keep him warm.
12. Great Uncle Bulgaria has two pairs of what?

DOWN

1. Which Womble finds reading and writing difficult?
2. What country did the wisest and oldest Womble choose as a name?
3. Wellington is very fond of _ _ _ _ _ _ _ as well as inventing things.
4. Tomsk, the nightwatch Womble, was once frightened by an _ _ _ that hooted at him on the common one night.
5. Do The Wombles think Human Beings are very untidy?
7. Great Uncle Bulgaria, Tobermory, Orinoco, Bungo, Tomsk, Madame Cholet, Alderney, and Wellington together make up the _ _ _ _ _ _ _
8. What is the missing word in this sentence? Madame Cholet likes _ _ cook.
10. The Wombles do not like these animals.
11. In the summer the Wombles love to go to the _ _ _ side.

Answers on page 60

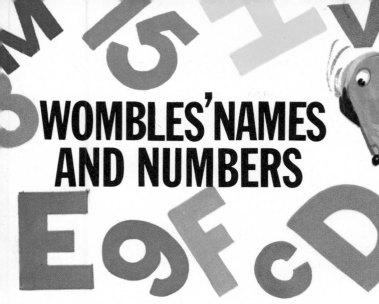

WOMBLES' NAMES AND NUMBERS

If A represents 1, B=2, C=3, and so on, can you puzzle out these number names of well-known Wombles:

$25 + 5 + 12 + 12 + 15 + 23 + 19 + 20 + 15 + 14 + 5 =$

$3 + 8 + 15 + 12 + 5 + 20 =$

$2 + 21 + 14 + 7 + 15 =$

$20 + 15 + 13 + 19 + 11 =$

$2 + 21 + 12 + 7 + 1 + 18 + 9 + 1 =$

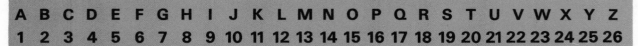

A	B	C	D	E	F	G	H	I	J	K	L	M	N	O	P	Q	R	S	T	U	V	W	X	Y	Z
1	2	3	4	5	6	7	8	9	10	11	12	13	14	15	16	17	18	19	20	21	22	23	24	25	26

Check your Answers on page 60

Hidden Wombles

Puzzle out these word and picture clues and you'll find the names of three Wombles hiding here.

Answers on page 60

(1st LETTER)

"Well, well" said Madame Cholet, putting on her gloves. "Will you all be good Wombles while I am away?"

"As good as gold," said Bungo. "But please don't stay away too long on your holiday. We shall miss you."

"We shall miss you like anything," agreed Orinoco, who is the greediest of the Wombles, and he sighed very loudly. A whole ten days with no Madame Cholet to do the cooking. It was a dreadful thought. They might even starve to death. Orinoco shivered violently.

"I have left you plenty of food in the larder and in the deep freeze," said Madame Cholet, "so you will have nothing to worry about. Now

MADAME CHOLET TAKES A TRIP.

I must hurry, or I shall miss my train, and then I shall miss the boat to France, which would never do. Au revoir, my little ones."

Off went Madame Cholet in the Wombles' own car, the Silver Womble, with Tobermory driving it. The last the others saw of her was a lacy handkerchief being waved out of the window.

"I wonder what these French Womble cousins Madame Cholet is going to stay with are like," said Wellington.

"Very French, I expect," said Tomsk in his slow voice. "I expect they even speak in French!"

"Well of course they do, you silly young Womble," said Great Uncle Bulgaria. "Now then, while Madame Cholet is away on holiday I think we should all plan a lovely surprise for her on her return."

"What sort of surprise?" asked Bungo.

"We shall spring-clean the kitchen, the larder and the deep freeze room," replied Great Uncle Bulgaria. "Everybody go and get an apron, a bucket and a mop and we will start work immediately!"

"Are you *sure* Madame Cholet will be pleased?" asked Orinoco. "She doesn't like it if we start changing things in her kitchen, you know."

"OF COURSE SHE WILL BE PLEASED," said Great Uncle Bulgaria in the voice which meant, 'stop arguing and do as you are told'. "Now, get a move on."

By the time Tobermory returned in the Silver Womble, the burrow was full of pails and buckets and mops and brooms and the smell of soapy water. As Tobermory was very hungry after his long drive he had been expecting a much nicer smell – dinner cooking. But when he tried to ask what was happening he was 'shushed' by Great Uncle Bulgaria and given a rather dry grassbread sandwich spread with buttercup mix, and told to go and help scrub down the walls of the larder.

"I wanted something *hot* to eat," grumbled Tobermory. "It's been a very long drive, you know, and the traffic was. . . ." But he was speaking to the empty air, for Great Uncle Bulgaria was already hurrying off towards the kitchen with a broom over one shoulder and a dustpan and brush in the other paw.

"Oh, I *shall* be glad when Madame Cholet gets back," muttered Tobermory.

He was not the only Womble to

use these words, for during the next few days they were repeated over and over again. Of course, all the Wombles had known that they were going to miss Madame Cholet – who is probably the best Womble cook in the whole world – but none of them had realised until now just how much they needed her. Naturally she had left behind a great many delicious deep frozen meals, such as moss pie with bracken topping, and clover and elmbark stew flavoured with fried toadstools, but somehow they just didn't taste the same. This may have been partly due to the fact that none of the

Wombles, not even Orinoco, seemed to remember the right time to get the food into the cooker.

"It's not my fault," said Bungo who, for once, was not at all bossy as all the others looked at him sadly over a rather soggy pie. "I thought I'd done the cooking right."

"Well you haven't," snapped Great Uncle Bulgaria, who was really getting very short-tempered these days, "and I *was* looking forward to a really melt-in-the-mouth pie. Oh well, well, it can't be helped, I suppose. Perhaps tomorrow will be better when Orinoco is in charge of the cooking."

But it wasn't; indeed, if anything, the supper was even worse. For Orinoco, who was feeling hungry all the time these days, had been so anxious not to *under*cook that he had *over*cooked. The result was a very black, smoky stew which even he couldn't finish up.

"Oh, I shall be glad when Madame Cholet gets back," said Tomsk and Wellington together.

"I shall be glad when all the spring-cleaning is finished," said Tobermory. "Well, let's get on with it . . ."

Actually the spring-cleaning was done very well and thoroughly so that, by the time Madame Cholet was due back, the kitchen, the larder and the deep freeze room were looking spick and span and as good as new. It was just the Wombles who were looking not very good. Their fur was no longer soft and sleek, their round little eyes were dull and, worst of all, they actually looked *almost thin!*

Everybody lined up outside the burrow front door to welcome Madame Cholet home, and there was a simply tremendous cheer as the Silver Womble drove up and out she got. Packed into the back of the car were three ENORMOUS cardboard boxes and, once Madame Cholet had spoken to everyone and been patted on the back and hugged and had her paw shaken over and over again, she asked for these mysterious boxes to be taken into the kitchen immediately.

"And then," said Madame Cholet, taking off her gloves and putting on her frilly overall, "I want nobody in my kitchen at all until supper-time! *Alors,* how beautifully you have painted and cleaned everything. *Tiens! Quelle surprise!"*

"There you are," said Tomsk, "I knew she'd talk all French when she came home. I told you so! Cor . . . that smells lovely . . . but different!"

And so it did, for that evening Madame Cholet dished up a lovely super, extra-delicious French Womble supper with the compliments of the Wombles of Boulogne, some of the Wombles' French cousins.

It certainly *was* a bit different, as

they had garlic dried grass paté and then casserole Française followed by Bombe Buttercup. It was a meal never to be forgotten – especially by Orinoco.

"Oh, we HAVE missed you, Madame Cholet," he said that evening as with all the others he sat at the now-empty table with his fur all soft and sleek, his little eyes shining and his stomach round and fat. "Please don't go away again for a long, long, LONG, time!"

"*Alors, tiens* and *quelle surprise*," said Madame Cholet. "No, I won't. Because – to tell you the truth – I have missed all of you!"

43

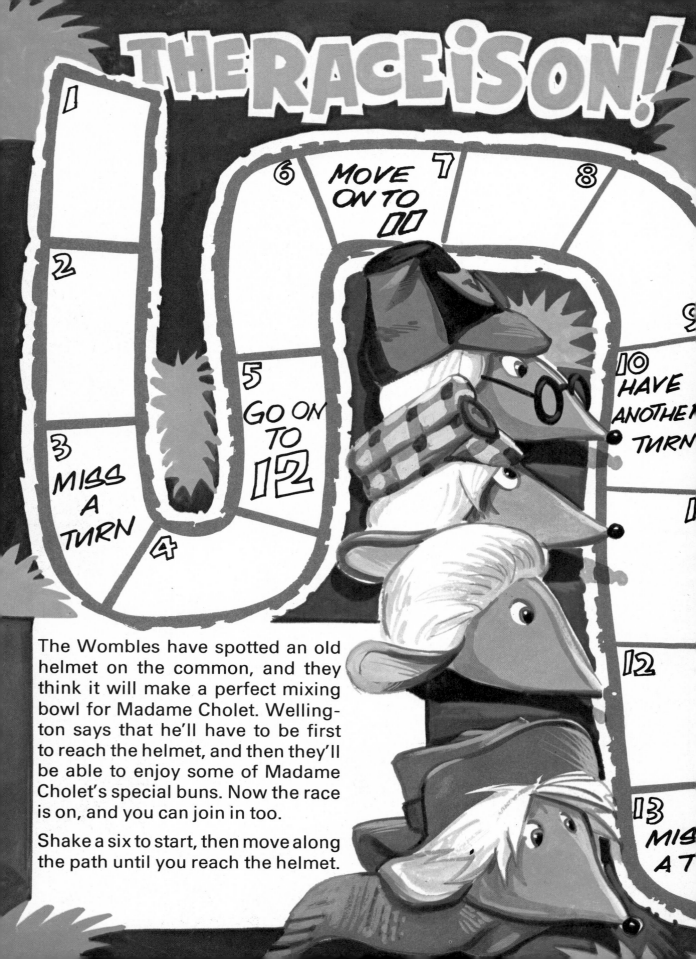

THE RACE IS ON!

The Wombles have spotted an old helmet on the common, and they think it will make a perfect mixing bowl for Madame Cholet. Wellington says that he'll have to be first to reach the helmet, and then they'll be able to enjoy some of Madame Cholet's special buns. Now the race is on, and you can join in too.

Shake a six to start, then move along the path until you reach the helmet.

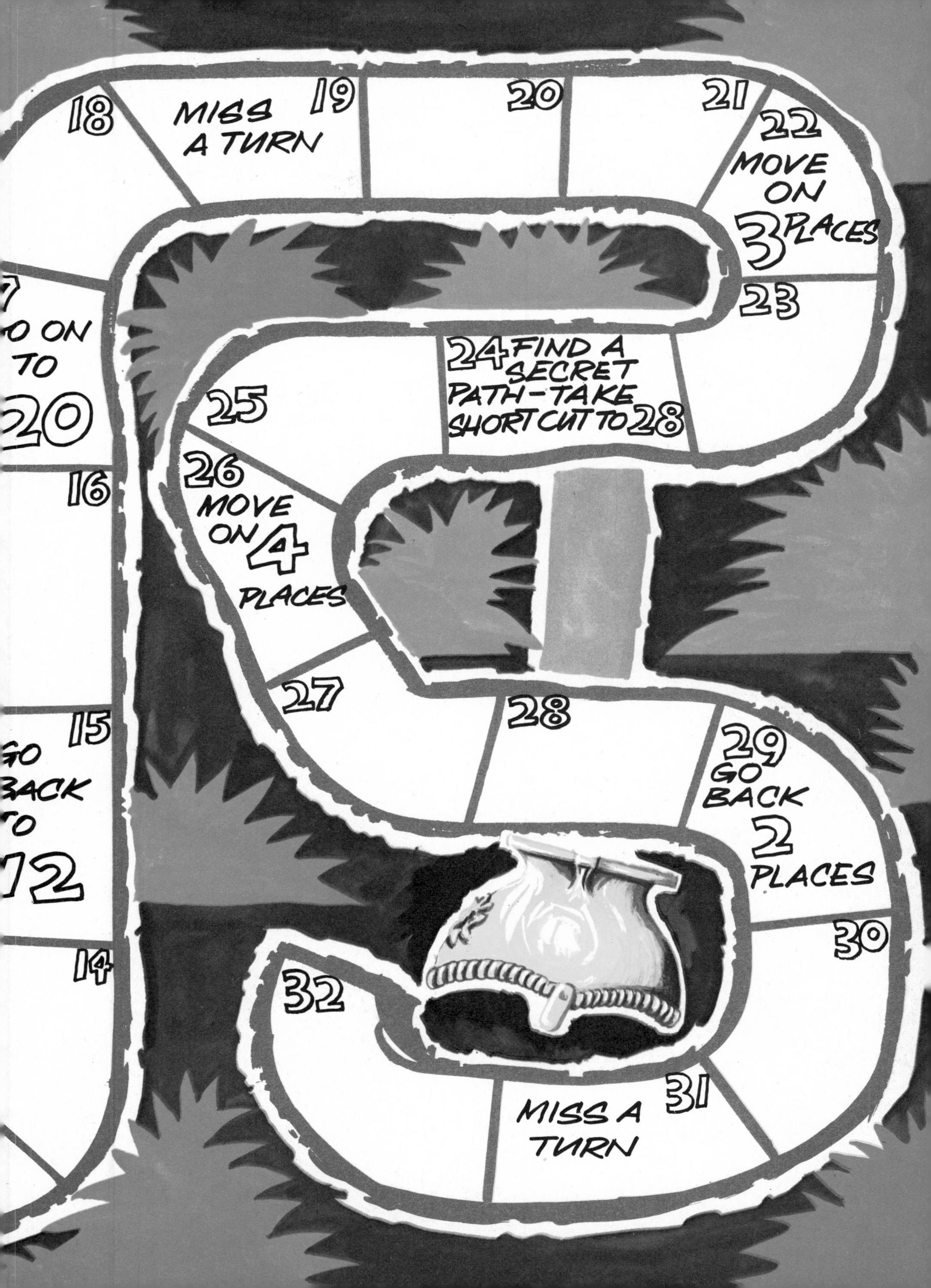

18

19 MISS A TURN

20

21

22 MOVE ON 3 PLACES

23

17 GO ON TO 20

24 FIND A SECRET PATH - TAKE SHORT CUT TO 28

25

16

26 MOVE ON 4 PLACES

15 GO BACK TO 12

27

28

29 GO BACK 2 PLACES

14

32

30

31

MISS A TURN

The Wombles help Father Christmas

"It's going to be a very cold Christmas this year. I shouldn't be at all surprised if it snows quite soon," said Great Uncle Bulgaria as he looked out of the Womble burrow on Wimbledon Common.

He pulled his MacWomble tartan shawl more closely round his shoulders and shivered, for the wind was *extremely* cold and Great Uncle Bulgaria is *extremely* old and his paws get rather chilly these days.

Of course Great Uncle Bulgaria was quite right – he always is! – and that night it snowed and snowed and SNOWED, so that by the time all the young Wombles, who had been out tidying up, got back to the burrow they all looked like Snow Wombles. They came stamping into the nice warm cosy home, swinging their arms and slapping their paws together, all of them talking at once, because they were very excited about it being Christmas time.

"The snow looks just like lovely icing on a cake," said Orinoco, who was carrying a large red lantern which he had found under a bush. "I think I won't eat anything at all on the day before Christmas, so that I can eat twice as much on Christmas Day!"

"You greedy young Womble," said Tobermory, who was neatly putting their things away in the Workshop. "You're far too fat as it

"*Ho hum*," said Great Uncle Bulgaria, who had just come into the Workshop, "is it indeed? *You've* only got a few pieces of wood in your paws, young Bungo. Tomsk is carrying FAR more than you are! *Brrrrrr*, what a very cold night it is, to be sure!"

And Great Uncle Bulgaria drew his MacWomble tartan shawl even more tightly round his shoulders.

"It's cold in here, because somebody has left the front door open," said Tobermory. "Dear me! What have we here?"

Everybody stopped talking and looked down the burrow to where a small, white figure was turning round and round saying. "I'm lost, I'm lost. I can't see anything, I'm lost. HELP!"

It was Wellington, the smallest and the shyest of the Wombles, whose spectacles were covered with snow so that he couldn't see where he was going. But the warmth of the burrow was melting the snow and making it go SPLIT SPLAT SPLUT on the floor. Clasped in Wellington's paws was a large round bucket.

"It's all right, Wellington old Womble, you're safely home," said Orinoco. "And, I say, what have you tidied up? IT LOOKS LIKE A BUCKET OF DELICIOUS BLACK TREACLE!"

"Treacle? Nothing of the kind, don't taste it, Orinoco!" said Tobermory.

But he was too late, for greedy Orinoco had already put his paw

is. What you need is more exercise, like helping Father Christmas. Father Christmas has to work *extremely* hard at this time of year, and with all this snow about, his job will be more difficult than ever!"

"We work jolly hard too!" said Bungo in his bossy way. "Look what Tomsk and I have tidied up. A lot of pieces of wood all tied together with wire and bits of string. It's very heavy to carry!"

into the bucket and was now licking it and making faces.

"Serves you right, you greedy young Womble," said Great Uncle Bulgaria, quite forgetting to feel chilly as he laughed. "It's not treacle at all, it's tar! What you have all been so busy clearing up are some old roadworks. First there was the lantern, then the fence that went round the roadworks and finally the bucket of tar the human beings must have been using! *Tck, tck, tck,* what careless, untidy creatures they are!"

"It tastes horrible," said Orinoco, screwing up his face more than ever and then wiping his mouth with the end of his red scarf.

"Well, it's not meant to be eaten," said Great Uncle Bulgaria. "Dear me, dear me. What a terrible night it is going to be for poor Father Christmas with all this snow!"

"I thought he was used to snow, because he lives at the North Pole, doesn't he?" asked Wellington, who now looked more his old self and less of a Snow Womble.

"Yes indeed, but it will be *extremely* difficult for him to find his way through this blizzard. You may have noticed that even the aeroplanes have stopped flying because of the weather, so it's going to be a very hard struggle for Father Christmas to make his rounds! *Tck, tck, tck.*"

At these words all the young Wombles looked at each other with their mouths going right down at the corners, because it seemed that perhaps they might not get all the presents they'd been hoping for. And, of course, it wasn't very nice to think of poor old Father Christmas bumping about in the blizzard and getting lost!

"I know what we'll do," said Tobermory, smacking his paws together. "We'll light up a nice, bright signal for him. Come along young Wombles."

Ten minutes later the door of the burrow opened and out marched all the Wombles, Great Uncle Bulgaria leading them with the red lantern, which was now shining brightly.

The snow was driving right across the Common like a great white

blanket, but as all the Wombles were roped together, nobody was frightened of getting lost. They all remembered exactly what Tobermory had told them to do and they all counted their footsteps under their breath, and when each of them had reached the exact right number, he stopped, and as each of them was holding a piece of wood with one tarry end and one sharp end, they pushed the sharp end into the snow and then waited patiently.

Up at the front Tobermory, by the light of the lantern, was looking first at his watch and then at his map of the Common in a very anxious way.

Great Uncle Bulgaria, in spite of the driving snow and the cold wind, wasn't worried at all. He just put his head on one side and listened, and then he said calmly: "Here he comes, Tobermory, I can hear him."

"Well, if you say so," said Tobermory, a bit doubtfully. "But I can't hear a thing except this dratted wind. Right, off we go . . ."

And Tobermory put a small piece of tarred wood into the lantern flame, until it spluttered and then caught fire and began to burn a beautiful clear red.

Off went Tobermory and although he is not the youngest of Wombles he walked *extremely* fast, and in a very short time indeed stick after stick caught fire from his torch, and soon, despite the driving snow *and* the tearing wind, right across the Common there appeared a great fiery arrow pointing the way to the centre of London.

Down below, the Wombles narrowed their little eyes as they held onto their torches and looked up at the sky, but all *they* could see were the whirling snowflakes and all *they* could hear was the roar of the wind. But Great Uncle Bulgaria seemed to see and hear something just a little bit extra, and he smiled and waved one white paw as just for a second a long dark shape appeared, flying across the black and white sky . . . .

"Dear me," said Great Uncle Bulgaria to himself, "Father Christmas doesn't seem a day older . . not a day! *Tck, tck, tck!*

The torches burnt out very quickly and everybody – still securely roped together – responded to a tug from his fellow Womble and trooped back to the burrow. They were *extremely* cold and rather tired and not at all sure that they really *had* helped Father Christmas to find his way across the Common.

But the next morning at the bottom of each bed every single Womble found *exactly* the present he most wanted . . . and what was more Great Uncle Bulgaria had a beautiful new thick tartan shawl which had pinned to it this message:

Thank you old friend. Good to see you again, even if it was only for a moment or two. Best wishes to you and all the Wombles for the New Year. Father Christmas.

"How *extremely* kind of him, when he's so busy," said Great

Uncle Bulgaria as he put on the new shawl. It was so warm and cosy he decided to go out and see what the weather was like after the stormy night.

The sun was shining, the sky was blue and there were Wombles everywhere, tobogganing, throwing snowballs and making Snow Wombles. And the biggest and best Snow Womble was wearing spectacles and had a stick and was wearing a very old MacWomble tartan shawl. It had been made by Bungo, Orinoco, Tomsk and Wellington.

"*Tck, tck, tck,* and very handsome too," said Great Uncle Bulgaria. "A happy Christmas, young Wombles." And he laughed and laughed all the way back to the burrow.

WHO'S HIDING?

To find out who's hiding, fill in the names of the objects numbered 1 – 7 in the boxes below. Now look down the first column and you'll find your hidden Womble friend! Who is it?

Answers on page 60

53

WIN A WOMBLE

A Super Competition to Give You the Chance of Owning A Womble of Your Own

Get your pens, pencils and crayons at the ready, because there are four fantastic Womble pyjama cases to be won by the lucky winners of this free competition. Two pyjama cases will be given to entrants in the 4-7 age group and two more to the entrants in the 7-11 age group, so don't forget to put your age on your entry, together with your name and address, of course! And for the runners-up in each group we've got some prizes too, we'll be giving away 20 Wombles Big T.V. Books.

All you have to do is write down the countries from which each of our Wombles shown here have taken their names, and we've dressed them in that country's national costume to give you a little extra help. Then, simply trace the large Womble outline our artist has drawn for you on tracing paper, or greaseproof paper will do, colour it and send it to us with your answers.

Send your entries to:

Win a Womble Competition,
World Distributors (Manchester) Ltd.,
P.O. Box 111,
12 Lever Street,
Manchester M60 1TS.

to reach us not later than 31st March 1976.
Winners will be notified, by post, at the
end of April.

DON'T FORGET **YOUR NAME**
YOUR ADDRESS
YOUR AGE

and, of course, your competition entry!

So now you've got all the details, the rest
is up to you. Good Luck!

TOBERMORY INVENTS A NEW MACHINE

Tobermory was really getting so overworked that he didn't know what to do next. The Wombles kept on coming into his Workshop asking for new Tidy-bags, and he just hadn't got enough to go round, as all the baskets and plastic bags they normally used were worn out.

"I don't know what to do," said Tobermory, scratching his head. "I suppose I'll just have to invent something! But what can possibly take the place of good old Tidy-bags?"

It was a very difficult problem and he was still thinking about it when Orinoco brought a very odd-looking object into the Workshop.

"I found it under a bush," said Orinoco. "What is it, Tobermory?"

Tobermory looked at the object, and turned it over and examined it again, and then he said: "I believe it must be a machine that Human Beings use for sucking in some of the rubbish they leave in their streets. It's called a road cleaner and it works off electricity. You push in

this little knob here and it goes *whoosh . . .* I'll show you!"

Tobermory pushed the little knob, but all that happened was that the machine made a groaning-grinding sound and then stopped.

"Dear me," said Tobermory. "It's not working properly. I'll have to mend it. Leave it with me, Orinoco. It may be just what we need!"

"I remember what happened last time we found a vacuum carpet cleaner thing," said Wellington. "Tobermory tried to mend that, too, and it didn't suck up rubbish – it blew it out. All over everything!"

"I heard that, young clever-sticks-Womble," said Tobermory. "Perhaps *you* think you could make it work better than I can. *Hum*?"

"No, rather not, Tobermory. Sorry," said Wellington, and he went trotting off after Orinoco to see if it was tea-time yet.

However, Wellington's words seemed to have jogged Tobermory's memory, and he appeared determined not to make the same mistake again. So this time he took the street cleaner to bits and he spread the parts all over the table in the Workshop and tried to work out what each did – or was supposed to do. It was such a long job that he missed his tea altogether and Madame Cholet came to see what was happening.

"You work much too hard," said Madame Cholet, waving a wooden spoon at Tobermory. "And you need proper meals or you will be ill. I shall bring you in a little snack. If I had *my* way . . ." and Madame Cholet went off muttering to herself.

What Madame Cholet would have liked to do Tobermory didn't know and, anyway, he had enough to worry about already with the rubbish mounting up all round him and out on the Common.

The next morning, as Wellington and Orinoco, Tomsk and Bungo were walking slowly through the burrow after a large and delicious breakfast of sizzling hot clover spread on fried grass bread, followed by warm moss buns with golden buttercup and wild honey, Tobermory, looking very tired, appeared in the Workshop doorway wheeling before him the 'street cleaner'.

"*Oi*," said Tobermory, trying not to yawn, "I've got something for you four young Wombles. The new, improved, better-than-ever-before Common-Cleaner. This is it!"

It was a most unusual looking machine, rather like a child's scooter with an enormous black plastic bag at the front. The bag had brushes all round the bottom of it, and attached to one side was a length of pipe with a nozzle on the end.

"Isn't it smart?" said Tobermory proudly as he gave his fearsome looking machine an affectionate pat. There is nothing like somebody inventing or mending or adapting something to make them feel that it is one of the most handsome objects in the whole world.

As Tomsk, Wellington and Bungo had not had a paw in creating this new sort of machine, and Orinoco had only found it when it looked very different, they did not feel the same way about it. In fact, to them it looked really rather frightening. It seemed, somehow, to be frowning at them. It even looked as though it might suddenly jump forwards and

growl or howl in a most scaring way.

"You see this red knob here?" went on Tobermory, who hadn't realised that the four young Wombles weren't as keen on the Common Cleaner as he was. "Well, you push that and this machine will suck in all the rubbish in its path. I've tried it out on the wood shavings on my Workshop floor and now the whole floor is ABSOLUTELY CLEAN! There's not a scrap of anything ANYWHERE."

"Oh dear . . ." said Wellington, who was always the most nervous of the younger Wombles. "Are you sure that it's safe, Tobermory?"

"Course it's safe. Don't be a cowardy-buttercup-young-Womble. Off you go. *Yooooo*!" said

Tobermory, and this time he *did* yawn, and so widely that he had to take off his bowler hat to try and politely cover the yawn. "Off, off, off. . . ." And he waved the bowler hat at them and went shuffling along to the kitchen and had a breakfast-cum-supper and, because he was so tired, he went straight to bed after his meal and fell very fast asleep indeed. Which was probably just as well, because he slept right through what happened next.

It was Tomsk, who is probably the bravest of the young Wombles, who got up the courage to press the little red button on the machine when he saw a pile of rubbish ahead on the Common. There was a tremendous roaring, scrunching noise and, as if by magic, all the rubbish was sucked into the big plastic bag. The bag swelled up for a moment, went *munch munch munch* and then got thinner.

"Oh my," said Orinoco," all those dirty, muddy bus tickets and bits of paper have VANISHED. I say, this is going to make work a lot easier, you know. It's my turn now. Hang on, I'll use that nozzle thing on that old cardboard box over there. . . ."

Whizzwooooosh!

"*Yoooooooooooow*!" yelled Orinoco. For away had gone his red scarf and his hat. They too had vanished into the Common-Cleaner and, what was more, Orinoco was being drawn towards it with all his fur being pulled to one side, so that he

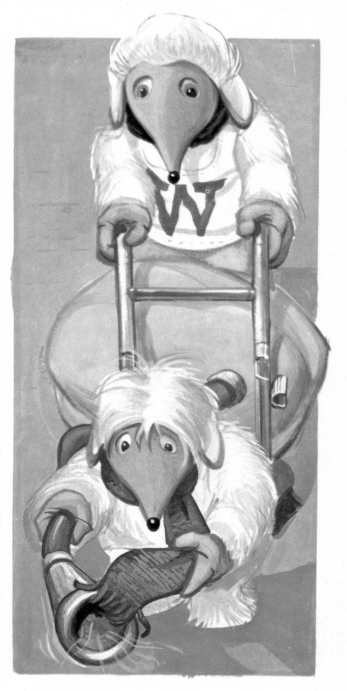

looked like a fat little Womble who had been caught in a Force 12 gale at the very least.

"*HEEEEEEEEEELP*!" shouted Orinoco. . . .

Bungo rushed to help him and . . .
WHIZZ WOOOOOOOOSH!
Away went Bungo's cap.

"*HEEEEEEEEELP*!" shouted Bungo.

Wellington ran to do what he could: which was to hang on to Bungo who was holding on to Orinoco. *All* their fur looked as if they had been caught in a Force *13* gale.

Away went Wellington's spectacles AND his cap AND his scarf....

"*Yooooooooow,*" yelled Wellington.

So, of course, Tomsk let go of the Common-Cleaner – which was now making the most dreadful howling noise – and the next thing HE knew was that his sports shirt was being pulled over his head, and then it too had vanished into the roaring machine.

What would have happened next nobody can tell, but luckily Great Uncle Bulgaria came out of the burrow at this point and, after one look at what was happening, he went over and pressed the red button on the machine, and the roaring and grinding stopped and Orinoco, Bungo, Wellington and Tomsk all fell in a heap.

"*Tut, tut, tut!*" said Great Uncle Bulgaria. "It seems to me that this machine is a little TOO efficient. Perhaps we had better put it away until the snow comes. I'm sure it will be SUPERB as a snow-cleaner-upper. But for the moment I believe it would be better to keep it at the very far end of the burrow. Now, young Wombles, pick yourselves

ANSWERS

ALL ABOUT THE WOMBLES
1. Great Uncle Bulgaria 2. Tobermory 3. Tomsk 4. Alderney 5. Orinoco 6. Yellowstone 7. Bungo 8. Coburg 9. An umbrella, a blackcurrant cake and six white handkerchiefs. 10. Quetta

WELLINGTON'S CROSSWORD
Across
1. Tobermory 6. Atlas 8. Two 9. Orinoco 11. Shawl 12. Spectacles

Down
1. Tomsk 2. Bulgaria 3. Reading 4. Owl 5. Yes 7. Wombles 8. To 10. Dogs 11. Sea

WOMBLES' NAMES AND NUMBERS
Yellowstone, Cholet, Bungo, Tomsk, Bulgaria

HIDDEN WOMBLES
1. Wellington, 2. Orinoco, 3. Tobermory

WHO'S HIDING?
1. Orange; 2. Rabbit; 3. Igloo; 4. Nest; 5. Owl; 6. Camel; 7. Oak. The Womble who's hiding is ORINOCO.

WHERE IN THE WORLD?

Great Uncle Bulgaria	–	Bulgaria
Wellington	–	New Zealand
Orinoco	–	Venezuela
Tobermory	–	Canada
Bungo	–	Japan
Cholet	–	France
Alderney	–	Britain
Tomsk	–	Russia

up, go and get four sharp pointed sticks from the Workshop and clear up the Common with them. You see, I think Madame Cholet has solved the problem of how to deal with clearing up all the extra rubbish!"

Great Uncle Bulgaria looked over his spectacles, his little round eyes twinkling.

"What is her idea?" asked Wellington, blinking short-sight-edly.

"That all you young Wombles should collect enough rubbish weight for weight with what you eat. So, if you only clear up and make use of small amounts, you will only get small amounts of breakfast, dinner and tea. All right?"

Orinoco heaved an enormous sigh and nodded. So did Tomsk, Bungo and Wellington. Then they pushed the Common-Cleaner back into the burrow very, very quietly. Tobermory didn't even stir in his sleep for another twelve hours. But when he heard about the new plan he smiled under his grey moustache and hummed under his breath.

Tobermory is really a very, very clever Womble.

P.S. Tomsk got his shirt back; Wellington his scarf, cap and spectacles (unharmed); Bungo his cap; Orinoco his hat and scarf. And the Common-Cleaner was MARVELLOUS at clearing up the snow!

WHERE IN THE WORLD?

All the Wombles agree that one of their favourite Midsummer Eve parties was the one where they all dressed up to represent the countries from which they'd chosen their names. During the party they held a competition to see if they could guess which country each of the